LEGO® MEDIEVAL ADVENTURES

Troll Attack

By Allison Lassieur

Illustrated by Mada Design, In[c.]

SCHOLASTIC INC.

NEW YORK   TORONTO   LONDON   AUCKLAND
MEXICO CITY   NEW DELHI   HONG KONG   BUENOS AIRES

ISBN-13: 978-0-545-09337-8
ISBN-10: 0-545-09337-6

LEGO, the LEGO logo, the Brick and the Knob configuration and the Minifigure are trademarks of The LEGO Group. © 2009 The LEGO Group. All rights reserved. Published by Scholastic Inc.
SCHOLASTIC and associated logos are trademarks and/or registered trademarks of Scholastic Inc.

12 11 10 9 8 7 6 5 4 3   9 10 11 12 13 14/0

Printed in the U.S.A.   23
First printing, February 2009

"Take that, troll!"
   Sir Gavin swung his sword at the troll in front of him. *BAM!* The troll was knocked to the ground. Another green troll rushed forward. Sir Gavin attacked. Soon the troll ran away.

The battle was over. Sir Gavin grinned. King Edward's army had won the battle against the evil wizard Morax and his troll army!

King Edward rode his horse onto the battlefield. The knights gathered around him. "Hooray for King Edward!" shouted the knights.

"Morax sent his trolls to capture the castle," King Edward said. "Once again, he is defeated!"

Suddenly a burst of light and smoke filled the battlefield. The evil wizard appeared.

"I have not lost," Morax shouted. "My army will return, and you will lose!" *CRACK!* Morax disappeared.

King Edward looked at his knights. "We must find out when the troll army will attack," he said worriedly. "Who will volunteer for this dangerous mission?"

"I will!" Sir Gavin shouted.

"You must go into the Forbidden Forest," said the king. "Find out when and where the troll army will attack. Then report back to me."

"I won't fail," Sir Gavin said, bowing.

"Look for help near the Shadow Caves," the king said mysteriously.

Sir Gavin rode deep into the Forbidden Forest. The forest was dim and stuffy. No birds sang. Nothing moved.

The knight searched the forest for any signs of
the troll army. He looked near the Scary Swamp.

He searched the Gloomy Grove.

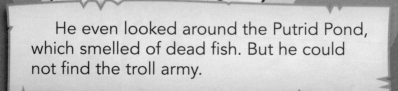

He even looked around the Putrid Pond, which smelled of dead fish. But he could not find the troll army.

Sir Gavin was discouraged. He did not want to fail King Edward. Then he remembered what the king had said about the Shadow Caves.

"What help can I possibly find there?" Sir Gavin said to himself. But he rode toward the caves anyway.

When he arrived, it was night. *It's too dark to search the caves,* Sir Gavin thought. *I will look in the morning.*

Suddenly a twig snapped. Sir Gavin drew his sword. "Who is there?" he shouted. "Speak!"

A cloaked figure stepped out of the shadows.

"Who are you?" Sir Gavin said.

The figure lifted the hood.
"Princess Alyssa!" Sir Gavin exclaimed. "I don't believe it!"
Princess Alyssa smiled. "Yes, it's me," she said.

Princess Alyssa and Sir Gavin sat down.
"I thought you were Morax's prisoner," Sir Gavin said.
"I have found a way to escape," Princess Alyssa said.
"Then why don't you?" Sir Gavin asked.
"This way," she said, "I can find out what he is up to."
"You are a spy!" Sir Gavin said.
The princess laughed. "Father doesn't want anyone to know," she said. "He must trust you very much."

19

Sir Gavin glowed with pride. "Do you have any news?" he asked.

"Yes," the princess said. "The troll army will attack at sunrise. And Morax is sending giant trolls."

Giant trolls! They were huge and strong. None of the king's weapons could defeat a giant troll.

"That is bad news," Sir Gavin said. He jumped up. "I must warn the king at once."

"Wait," the princess said.

She gave Sir Gavin a glass bottle filled with a blue liquid.

"This is a sleeping potion," she said. "I took it from Morax's workroom. A few drops will put a person to sleep."

"Does it work on trolls?" Sir Gavin asked.

"I don't know," Princess Alyssa said.

The princess pulled the hood over her face. "I must get back before the guards notice I am gone. Good luck!" She disappeared into the forest.

Sir Gavin raced back to the castle. When he arrived he went straight to the king. He gave the potion to the king. He told King Edward about meeting the princess. "My daughter is smart and brave," King Edward said proudly. "I hope her plan works."

By sunrise everything was ready. The king and his knights stood along the castle walls. Large catapults stood ready to shoot huge boulders at the troll army. "I hope this works," Gavin said.

A low rumble sounded in the distance. It grew louder. It was the troll army! Gavin gripped his sword. Sure enough, there were several giant trolls with the army. The massive army marched to the castle gate.

Suddenly a loud *CRACK!* filled the air. The evil wizard Morax appeared.

"Prepare to meet your doom!" he shouted at the king.

King Edward smiled. "We shall see," he said.

"Fire the catapults!" the king shouted. Several huge boulders flew through the air toward the troll army.

The giant trolls marched forward. One by one, they swung their clubs at the boulders. *BAM! BAM! BAM!* The boulders shattered like glass.

Morax laughed. "See!" he said. "You cannot defeat my army! The castle will be mine!"

A strange blue smoke rose from each piece of stone. Soon the battlefield was covered in blue fog.

One by one, the trolls sank to the ground. They began to snore. The giant trolls crashed to the ground. Their snoring was so loud that the castle walls shook.

ZZZZ

"Get up!" Morax shouted. He poked a giant troll with his staff. The troll yawned and rolled over. "Get up, I say!" Morax screamed. But it was too late.

"This is not over!" Morax said furiously. He waved his staff. The whole army disappeared with a *WHOOSH*. Then with a *CRACK!* Morax disappeared, too.

The king's army began to cheer. "Hooray!" shouted Sir Gavin.

"Well done, Sir Gavin," King Edward said. "We have defeated Morax once again, thanks to you and Princess Alyssa."